HELPING HANDS

HOW MONKEYS ASSIST PEOPLE WHO ARE DISABLED

TEXT AND PHOTOGRAPHS BY

SUZANNE HALDANE

DUTTON CHILDREN'S BOOKS

NEW YORK

The monkey handprints shown in this book are actual size.

My sincere thanks for the generous assistance of the following people: Jill Gelalia; Tom Hyman; Charlotte Ireland; Julia Lebentritt; Alice Levee; Michael, Sunny, and Zina Levin; Dan McCormack; Mary McDonald; Alison Pescoe; Cary Ryan; Maude Salinger; Beverly, Greg, and Thomas Slane; Sue Strong; David Taylor; Sydney Thomas; Sydney Thomson; Karen Tolman; Dr. M. J. Willard and the staff at Helping Hands; and Joe Williams.

Library of Congress Cataloging-in-Publication Data
Haldane, Suzanne.
Helping hands: how monkeys assist people who are disabled/text and photographs by Suzanne Haldane.—1st ed.
    p.   cm.
Summary: A photo essay focusing on a teenager with quadriplegia and his capuchin monkey, illustrating how capuchins are trained to provide help and companionship to people who are disabled.
    ISBN 0-525-44723-7
1. Monkeys as aids for the handicapped—Juvenile literature.
2. Capuchin monkeys—Juvenile literature.   3. Quadriplegics—Rehabilitation—Juvenile literature.   4. Physically handicapped teenagers—Rehabilitation—Juvenile literature.   [1. Monkeys as aids for the handicapped.   2. Monkeys—Training.   3. Capuchin monkeys.   4. Quadriplegics—Rehabilitation.   5. Physically handicapped—Rehabilitation.]   I. Title.
HV1569.6.H35   1991
362.4'383—dc20   90-27382   CIP   AC

Published in the United States by Dutton Children's Books, a division of Penguin Books USA Inc.

Printed in U.S.A.   First Edition   10 9 8 7 6 5 4 3 2 1

for Greg Slane and Sue Strong

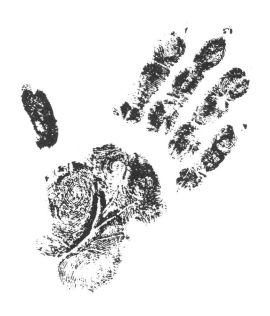

and for Ian—in his third year

This is Greg and his friend Willie. Willie is an adult female capuchin (kap' yŏo chin) monkey. She is both Greg's companion and his trained assistant.

Greg has a dog for a pet, but Willie is much more than a pet to Greg. Every day she is at his side to help him do many of the things that he can't do by himself.

Greg is a cheerful, friendly teenager who laughs easily. These days he spends his waking hours in a wheelchair, but it wasn't always so. Greg used to be extremely active, like most boys his age. He enjoyed wrestling and playing ball with his friends and going boating, camping, and fishing with his family.

One Memorial Day weekend his life changed dramatically. After a game of football, Greg and his friends went to a river. Eager to cool off, he swam out to a barge anchored in the water. When he dove off the barge, he hit his head on something several feet below the surface of the water.

He has a vivid memory of what happened next. "I couldn't get myself out of the water. I was able to float, but I couldn't swim. My friends saw that I was in trouble and pulled me to shore.

"I had no idea how badly I was injured. All I knew was that I couldn't move. One of my friends told me to relax. 'It's probably only a pinched nerve, and you'll be okay soon,' he said. But I had the feeling something more serious was wrong. I insisted they call an ambulance."

Greg was rushed to the hospital. After examining him, doctors told Greg's parents that he had broken his neck and injured his spinal column. His nerves were damaged. The delicate, fibrous network that sends messages to his brain could no longer instruct his muscles to lift and manipulate his arms and legs. He was paralyzed from the shoulders down. In one tragic instant he had become a quadriplegic—a person whose arms and legs are paralyzed. Someone can move Greg's limbs for him, but he can't move them himself.

Greg spent two and a half months in the hospital. Gradually he grew used to the new stillness of his body. He discovered how much he had taken the normal use of it for granted. For instance, when he has an itch, he can't scratch it. Someone has to do it for him. Something as simple as turning over in bed is also impossible—he needs help for that, too. He can still feel emotions and think, but he can't move from the shoulders down. He says his body feels as if it is encased in concrete.

"When I was told I'd be paralyzed the rest of my life, I became angry," Greg says. " 'How could I have done such a stupid thing?' I kept asking myself. I didn't know the area. I should have tested the depth of the water before diving in.

"After I got over the shock of what happened, I hoped there would be some medical breakthrough that could cure me. There were so many different people taking care of me, and there was so much being done to me, that I didn't have time to be sad. It wasn't until I was about ready to come home and pictured myself in familiar surroundings that I got depressed."

Friends tried to think of ways to lift Greg's spirits and make him laugh. One day they came to visit him in the hospital with their heads shaved. Laughing was one of the few things Greg could still do. He quickly realized that a sense of humor was a good weapon against his condition.

After the hospital stay, Greg spent nine months in a rehabilitation center. There he met other people with quadriplegia. Many of them had been injured in traffic accidents, falls, or sports activities such as football. In that setting he began to learn how to deal with his new life.

He was taught how to operate an electric wheelchair. By puffing his breath into the end of a horizontal tube that runs in front of his face and down one side of the chair to the motor between the back wheels, he could set the chair in motion without needing his hands.

He discovered that a lapboard was a useful addition to his wheelchair. It's a flat piece of thick plastic that rests across the arms of the chair. The board is a convenient place to rest his arms or to keep objects he may want to have right next to him—such as a cassette player.

Greg also learned a good way to operate a push-button telephone, cassette player, and computer. Holding a mouthstick—a rubber-tipped metal rod—between his teeth, he could move his head to push down buttons or keys.

Once he accepted his paralysis and had some experience with his changed body, Greg decided he wanted to be as independent as possible. Soon after the accident his mother had quit her job to take care of him, and the rest of his family were always ready to help. But Greg wanted to be able to get along without their aid for at least part of each day.

A representative from Easter Seals helped design Greg's wheelchair-accessible room. She told him that a psychologist named Dr. Mary Joan Willard was aiding people who have quadriplegia. She had been training monkeys to assist them with the routine tasks they were no longer able to perform.

After she earned her doctoral degree, Dr. Willard began working with people recovering from serious accidents. As a psychologist she helped them accept their disabilities and become adjusted to a new way of living.

In 1977 she began to work with a young man who had quadriplegia. She was stunned to discover how little he could do for himself.

Her involvement with someone who needed constant aid started Dr. Willard thinking about ways she could improve conditions for those in similar situations. Suppose an animal could be trained to be an affectionate assistant? Her first idea was to teach chimpanzees how to help people with disabilities.

She had been assisting B. F. Skinner, a behavioral psychologist known for his work in training animals by rewarding them with food when they performed correctly. But when she told Dr. Skinner of her plan, he reminded her that chimps grow to be at least 150 to 200 pounds and can be mean-tempered as adults. He suggested that she try capuchin monkeys.

Dr. Willard knew that monkeys are intelligent, have a natural curiosity, and are nearly as good at using their hands as humans are at using theirs.

She remembered seeing photos of organ-grinders—street musicians who play hand-cranked organs. Organ-grinders are usually accompanied by a small monkey who begs coins from passersby. And she had read that in Southeast Asia monkeys called pig-tailed macaques help harvest the coconut crop. On command, they shinny up trees and drop the coconuts to the ground. The coconuts are then gathered up and taken to market.

Dr. Willard consulted several primatologists—people who study monkeys and apes. They too recommended the capuchin. Its small size and attentive nature would be well-suited to her goal. Because they are skillful with their hands and can concentrate on solving problems, she hoped she could train them to help humans who have quadriplegia.

Capuchin monkeys like Willie come from Central and South America, and usually live to be at least thirty years old. Such long lives make them valuable companions.

Weighing only five to eleven pounds and standing about eighteen inches tall, capuchin monkeys are more manageable than larger primates such as chimpanzees. And capuchins have something chimps don't have—a tail they can manipulate almost as skillfully as their other four limbs. Their tails are helpful for carrying objects, for holding on to things, and just for keeping their balance when they are working or playing.

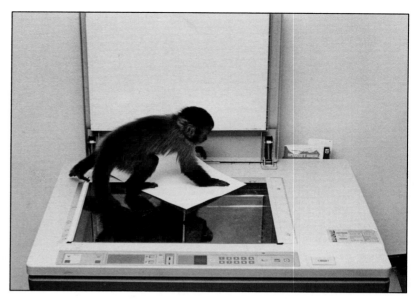

A capuchin's small hands and nimble fingers resemble human hands. They can unscrew jar lids, open doors, pick up a tiny piece of thread, and even hold a pencil and scribble.

Capuchins can also solve problems. One monkey in the wild seemed eager to open a clamshell and eat the clam. First the monkey picked up a stone and tapped the shell. Then it tried throwing the shell on the ground. Finally, it picked up a twig and pried the shell open.

Another monkey who lives with a human family was offered a spoonful of raw egg by a visiting friend. The monkey wanted the egg, but she was afraid to get too close to the visitor because she didn't know him. She cautiously approached the spoon with her arm fully extended in front of her body, dipped her hand in the egg, then ran to the far corner of the room to lick the egg off her hand.

Capuchins are clever as well. By watching people, this monkey has learned how to operate a photocopying machine. She can push the print button and catch the sheets of paper as they come out. She doesn't know how to place the paper on the glass, however.

Monkeys learn the same way human children do—by observing, imitating, and exploring.

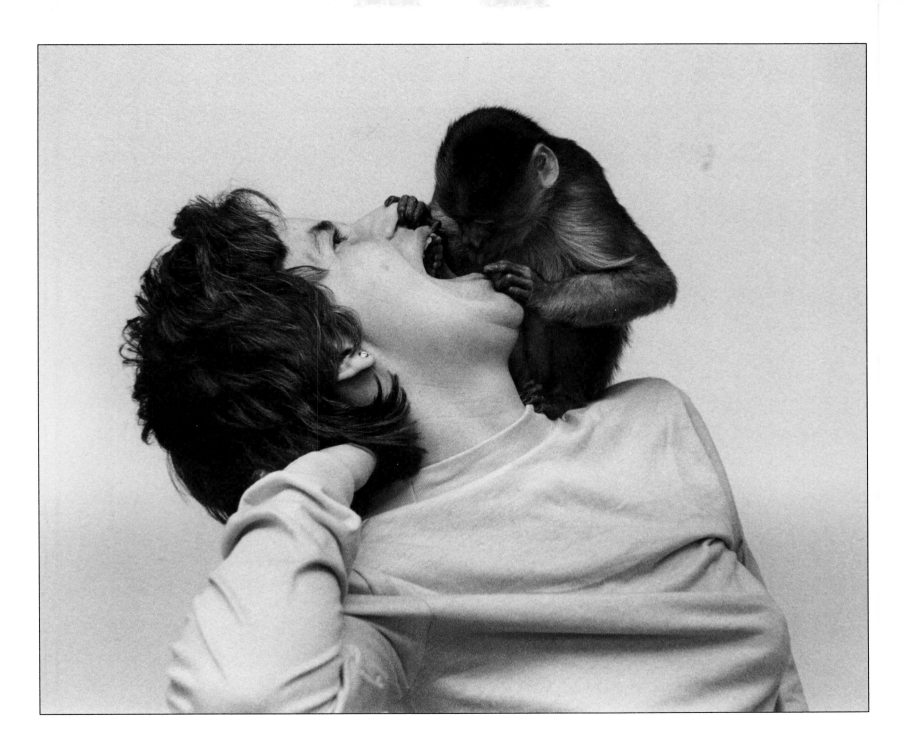

In 1977 Dr. Willard started research with a two-thousand-dollar grant and some of her own money. With that small sum she was able to buy four monkeys, some cages, and monkey food. She called her program Helping Hands.

Today Helping Hands is a nonprofit organization affiliated with Boston University's School of Medicine. It receives funding from private contributors and foundations. Dr. Willard hopes to be able to raise enough money to place forty to fifty monkeys with quadriplegics each year.

When she began Helping Hands, Dr. Willard called primate centers, zoos, and research facilities to let them know she needed capuchin monkeys. The first monkeys she received and trained were adults. Most were pets whose owners could no longer care for them. But some of the older monkeys had suffered abuse or neglect as pets or subjects of lab experiments, and they didn't completely trust humans.

She soon learned that baby capuchins raised by humans in foster homes become more affectionate adults, make better students, and adapt more easily to living with people than older capuchins who come to the project already set in their ways.

The monkeys now entering the Helping Hands project are born in a breeding colony at Disney World in Florida. At birth, infants weigh about nine ounces—the weight of an average-size apple.

Like the Seeing-Eye program, which places puppies with foster families until the puppies are old enough to be trained to help people who are blind, Helping Hands' monkeys live in foster homes. A member of Dr. Willard's staff carefully selects a volunteer foster home for a monkey to live in until it is about four years old. When a monkey is between six and eight weeks old and is strong enough to travel, it is flown directly to its new home.

To qualify for raising a monkey, members of a potential foster family must prove that they love and respect animals and can provide what the monkey needs. The family must have a great deal of time to devote to cuddling, playing with, and cleaning up after a monkey. Monkeys are as active as two-year-old human children. They

require a great deal more attention than a puppy or kitten.

Infant monkeys need to be fed every few hours from baby bottles. In the wild they nurse from their mothers, but in foster homes they drink a human baby formula that provides the nutrients necessary to keep them healthy and help them grow. When they are two months old, they can sleep through the night without anyone having to get up and give them a bottle. At this age, they get their first set of teeth and can also eat various kinds of fruit, such as grapes and pieces of apple. Between five and six months, baby monkeys are weaned from the bottle and are gradually introduced to an adult monkey diet.

In foster homes, or later at the training center, older capuchins eat about ten to twenty walnut-size monkey biscuits a day. These commercially prepared biscuits provide a nutritious diet. The adult capuchins also eat half an orange and—their favorite—a handful of grapes, or bits of other fruit. And every morning, like many human children, Helping Hands' monkeys get a chewable vitamin pill.

Monkeys also like to eat insects. But they have to catch those for themselves. Willie is especially good at reaching out both hands and snatching flies in midair. She doesn't like cockroaches, however.

In the wild, a female monkey grooms her baby daily. She picks through its fur to remove the insects, pieces of dirt, and dried skin that accumulate as the monkey travels through trees. Grooming is a pleasant activity for monkeys. They sit quietly and relax. Both the groomer and the one being groomed seem to enjoy the experience.

But a human care-giver gives a monkey a sponge bath instead. This monkey watches as his human friend demonstrates the motion of the damp washcloth on her own hand. The care-giver shows the capuchin what she's planning to do, so he won't become frightened when it's done to him.

Then it's the monkey's turn to be given a sponge bath. He probably feels as if he's being groomed, and he likes it.

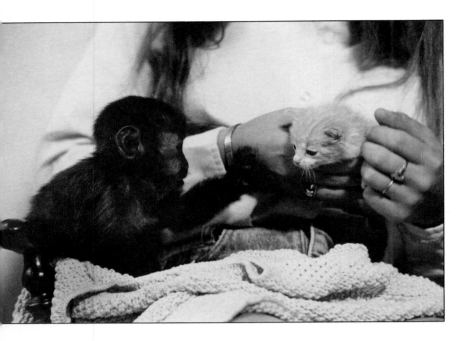

The foster family must keep its monkey healthy and safe, and give it a minimum of four hours of exercise outside the cage each day. They must also include it in the family routines and give it plenty of hugs and love. It's as important for monkeys to feel the warmth of physical contact with another being as it is for people.

Young foster monkeys can have a rich and stimulating experience in their temporary homes. They also become quite accustomed to accompanying their human parents outside the house, and behave as though it's natural for a monkey to do so. One foster parent lets her monkey hand the turnpike ticket to the ticket-taker whenever she's traveling. Another parent takes her monkey shopping. And still another reports that her monkey likes to ride on her dog's back whenever the three of them go walking in the park.

During the four years of a monkey's stay, a strong bond develops between the family, their pets, and the visiting capuchin. When the time comes for the monkey to separate from its foster family, it can be a sad experience for all. But soon the monkey is busy learning how to help a person who has quadriplegia, and the foster family takes pride in having played a part in Helping Hands' goal of placing affectionate monkeys with people who need them. Some foster families even volunteer to take care of another monkey.

When a monkey moves in to the training center, chances are it will interact with more people than it did in the foster home. One person usually trains the monkey, but various people take turns feeding, bathing, and playing with it.

Judi Zazula, a rehabilitation specialist who helps people in wheelchairs adapt their surroundings to a new way of life, works with Dr. Willard in the Helping Hands program. They are assisted by a dozen trainers. Most of them are college students. Some are studying psychology and believe the experience with monkeys will be helpful to their careers. Some plan to work with children who are developmentally disabled and know that a few of the techniques used in teaching monkeys are similar to those used with youngsters. And some simply love working with animals.

Dr. Willard and Ms. Zazula know it takes a special person to work with monkeys, and they select their staff carefully. "I like my trainers to be able to see things from the monkey's point of view. And he or she must have good problem-solving abilities and be able to change the way a task is being taught so that any monkey will be able to understand how to do it," Ms. Zazula says.

A trainer must have patience, sensitivity, insight, and, of course, a love for animals. Knowing when to allow a monkey to be careless in its lessons and when to insist that it be precise affects how well the monkey learns. And being sensitive to each monkey's unique personality—knowing its likes and dislikes—makes for a better, more productive training session.

"You have to think like a monkey," says one trainer. "And you can't be afraid to get down on the floor and get dirty. Monkeys will get food all over you."

Usually a trainer is assigned to one monkey and trains the animal every day. The monkey's lessons usually last about an hour. But each monkey has a pace at which it learns best, so lessons are geared to the needs of the individual.

About fifteen to twenty monkeys are in training at any one time. The entire learning process takes about six months to complete.

Initial training sessions take place in a small room or specially constructed cubicle. In a small space, the capuchin is less easily distracted, so it can pay greater attention to the lessons. Later the monkey will be taught in a room that is similar to the major living area of the person it will aid.

Teaching a monkey can be a challenge for a trainer. A monkey does not always perform a task just because someone asks it to. It must have its own good reason for wanting to cooperate.

A lick of fruit-flavored baby food or a dab of peanut butter are both good reasons. Positive reinforcement is used to encourage a monkey to participate. Dr. Willard's monkeys are taught by an animal-training technique known as "response and reward." Each time a capuchin makes the correct response, it is rewarded with a favorite food and the trainer's praise—"Good girl!" or "Good boy!" In time, the monkey will expect a treat for doing a task correctly.

In the first few days of training, a monkey learns how the response-and-reward system works. It is allowed to explore and play in the training room. Every few minutes the trainer rings a small countertop bell and immediately offers food—baby food to be licked off a finger, for instance. After several dozen repetitions, a capuchin has learned to expect food every time it hears the bell.

The trainer begins a lesson by showing the monkey what it is supposed to do. When the monkey performs the task correctly, the trainer rings the bell. If it makes a mistake, the bell is not rung and the monkey doesn't get a reward. Both the bell and the reward of food let the monkey know immediately that it has done what was wanted.

Further along in training, the bell is removed and the monkey learns that each time it is praised with the words "Good girl!" or "Good boy!" it will get a reward.

Like cats and dogs, monkeys learn to respond to certain simple words and gestures made by humans. So trainers always use the same combination of words when they want the monkey to perform a particular task. When a quadriplegic receives a monkey, he or she will be taught the specific verbal commands the monkey understands.

Helping Hands' monkeys begin their training by learning simple exercises. Just as a human baby must learn to crawl before he or she learns to walk, the simple things a monkey learns will help him or her to understand and perform more complicated tasks in the future.

At the training center, the first task a monkey learns is to fetch. The monkey is asked to pick up a simple object. Anything will do. Most of the time, Helping Hands' trainers use a rubber sink stopper, because it has a clear shape and is indestructible.

The trainer breaks each task down into easy steps and shows the monkey how to perform each one. Monkeys easily imitate human behavior, so it usually doesn't take long for the monkey to catch on.

As the trainer demonstrates a new part of the lesson, she speaks the name of the monkey and says, "Do this!"

First she shows the monkey how to place the stopper in a small box. It takes several days, about an hour each day, for the monkey to learn this. Then the trainer places her hand in the box and asks the monkey to place the stopper in her hand. Finally, she takes the box away, and the monkey is required to put the stopper in her hand. After the monkey has successfully performed that step—perhaps a dozen times on different days—it is ready to move on.

The last part of the lesson consists of a task that the monkey will actually perform for the person it will help. Someone from the center will sit in a wheelchair, pretending to have quadriplegia, and ask the monkey to fetch something that has fallen off his or her lapboard —a book, for instance. The person in the wheelchair will call the monkey by name, then say, "Fetch." The monkey will pick up the book and place it on the lapboard.

When the monkey has done this successfully, it's on its way to becoming true "helping hands."

People with quadriplegia cannot reinforce their verbal commands by using their arms or legs to show a monkey what they want done, so a way had to be devised to show the monkey which object to pick up, or fetch, and where to place it. Dr. Willard decided to try mounting a small laser near the mouth control that quadriplegics use to operate their electric wheelchairs.

The laser is in an eight-inch-long horizontal tube. Perpendicular to the tube, there's a control stick that's about three inches long and as thin as the lead in a pencil. A quadriplegic takes the end of the stick in his or her mouth and moves it around to control the movement of the laser. The laser projects a harmless beam of light that shows up as a red dot when it hits something. All the person has to do is aim it first at an object to be fetched, then at the spot to which the monkey should take the object.

Before a capuchin has its initial lesson with the laser, the monkey must get used to seeing it projected on different things. Its first instinct is to chase the little red dot of light. Some monkeys try to catch and eat it.

In this lesson, the trainer shines the laser on a bottle and tells the monkey to fetch it. If the monkey selects the correct bottle and brings it back to her trainer, she gets a grape as her reward. If she makes a mistake, she won't get a reward. But the trainer will give her as many chances as she needs to get it right.

People with quadriplegia often ask their monkeys to fetch and serve them something to drink. So one of the most helpful tasks a monkey learns is how to insert a straw into a container.

A monkey is first taught to put a two-inch straw into a container. When the animal becomes skilled in handling a short one, a slightly longer straw—say four inches long—will be substituted. Longer straws will be used as lessons progress.

This monkey has graduated to using an extra-long plastic straw. Once she learns how to put it into a container, she'll be taught to insert a flexible straw that is more convenient for a quadriplegic to use.

About halfway through training, a monkey is assigned to the person it will aid. Judi Zazula matches the personality and needs of the person with the temperament and capability of the monkey. Like people, some monkeys are better at doing one task than another. For instance, one monkey at the center was especially good at following the laser dot, but not so good at following verbal commands. Judi Zazula had a man with quadriplegia on her list who had suffered damage to the speech center of his brain and couldn't speak. The two were matched and are now working quite well together. When the man wants to get the monkey's attention before he points to something with his laser, he simply blows a whistle attached to his wheelchair.

A monkey is taught those tasks specifically requested by the person it will aid. The capuchin may learn to do any of the following:

> turn a light on or off
> open or close a door
> retrieve a dropped mouthstick
> fetch the remote control for a TV
> scratch an itch with a soft facecloth
> fetch a book or magazine
> fetch a videotape and position it for insertion into a VCR
> fetch an audiocassette and insert it into a cassette player
> fetch, position, and open a cold drink
> fetch and insert a computer disk
> let itself into its cage
> fetch a sandwich from a refrigerator, put it into a microwave oven, and transfer it to a feeding tray

Helping Hands teaches monkeys to do only the part of the task that a person can't. For instance, a monkey will insert an audiotape into a cassette player. Although a monkey can be taught how to work the machine, the quadriplegic will use a mouthstick to push the buttons that operate it.

There are no graduation ceremonies when a monkey finishes school. Instead of a diploma, it gets a new home and a person who is eager for help. "Most humans have pets to take care of," says one woman with quadriplegia. "But each of Helping Hands' monkeys has a person to take care of—someone who needs it a lot."

When Willie finished her training, she went to live with Greg. But before she arrived, Greg and his family had to make a few preparations for her.

A corner of Greg's room had to be rearranged to make space for Willie's cage. Standing seven feet tall, three feet wide, and three feet deep, the specially designed wire-mesh cage would serve primarily as Willie's bedroom.

Since Greg planned to have Willie serve him drinks, he had a small under-the-counter refrigerator installed in his room. A laser device and food dispenser were added to his wheelchair. The food dispenser would enable Greg to reward Willie for work well done.

Furniture and other objects that Greg didn't want Willie to touch or play with had to be marked. In her training, Willie was taught to stay away from anything with a white quarter-size sticker on it. So any of Greg's possessions that would be considered "out-of-bounds" for Willie were carefully marked with white stickers.

Willie learned that if she persisted in touching anything containing a white sticker—if she opened the medicine cabinet, which is full of drugs that could harm her—she would hear a high-pitched sound. When Greg needs to warn her, he presses a button on a small speaker attached to his wheelchair. The noise is

annoying to monkeys and makes them stop whatever they are doing. But humans are only mildly irritated by it.

When Greg's room was monkey-proofed, he was ready for Willie's arrival. Two years after his accident, he was looking forward to meeting the monkey that would share a large part of his life.

On the way to Greg's, Willie sat on the front seat of the car beside her trainer. Every now and then she got up on the back of the seat and looked out the car window. When they arrived at Greg's house, Willie climbed up on her trainer's shoulder and wrapped her tail around the young woman's neck so she wouldn't fall off as they walked into the house.

The trainer placed Willie immediately in her cage, knowing that the confinement would give Willie a sense of security. After a brief discussion with Greg, and a promise to return when the monkey felt at ease, Willie's trainer left.

Dr. Willard says it can take as little as a week or as long as a few months for a monkey to feel completely comfortable and to find its place in the family. The length of the adjustment period depends on the monkey's temperament.

"For about a week Willie didn't come out of her cage," says Greg. As a means of encouraging her to come out, she was offered food outside her cage. Invariably she grabbed it and ran back inside her safe quarters.

During Willie's period of adjustment, Greg's

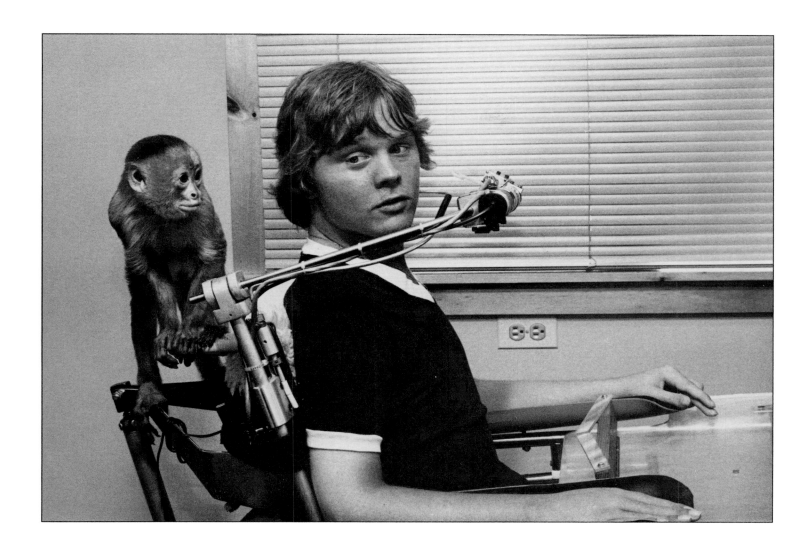

family gave her a rubber squeaky toy, which she held in her tail. Sometimes she insisted on taking it to bed with her.

Willie appears to be quite comfortable now and knows her routine. Her most frequent jobs are putting Greg's mouthstick back in his mouth when he drops it, serving him drinks, and fetching a book when he lets her know he wants one.

She is a wiry character. Her body almost resembles the animals children make from pipe cleaners. When she's in motion, her quick movements are exaggerated by her long, slender arms and legs.

She is not at all timid and can be quite forward with strangers. One day a woman visiting Greg was holding some color photographs. Willie went up to the woman, took hold of her arm, and shook it, apparently because she wanted the photos. No, not timid, and not always polite, either—that's Willie.

No one was certain how Willie would react to the family's pet dog, Trapper—a Doberman pinscher. As it turned out, it was the dog who initially had a problem with the relationship. Whenever she went up to Willie, the monkey

pushed her away. They're friends now, though. Trapper sniffs Willie, and the monkey ignores the dog.

Once Willie had settled down, her trainer came back to teach Greg how to give the simple verbal commands that Willie understands. Then Greg and Willie practiced working together.

Willie has good days and bad days. Like people, she has times when it just seems hard to get things right. Sometimes it can be tricky fitting an audiocassette into the player, but Willie tries again and again until she succeeds.

Greg is a determined individual. He insists on doing all that he can for himself. He operates his cassette player, computer, and push-button telephone with his mouthstick. He also uses it to turn the pages of a magazine or book. It's a helpful instrument, but it can easily slip out of his mouth. During long periods of work on the computer, Greg sometimes drops the stick.

When he does, he says, "Willie, fetch stick," and Willie picks it up and puts it back into his mouth.

"You should have seen Willie while she was learning how to give me the mouthstick. It didn't take her very long to get it right, but sometimes she put it in her own mouth. It was a funny scene!"

Greg is completing his education by computer. He had a specially designed tray fitted onto his display terminal so that Willie can help him when he uses his computer. He points to a floppy disk with his mouthstick and then taps the tray.

Willie picks up the disk and drops it into the tray. Greg uses his mouthstick to push the disk into the disk drive. Then he's ready to work.

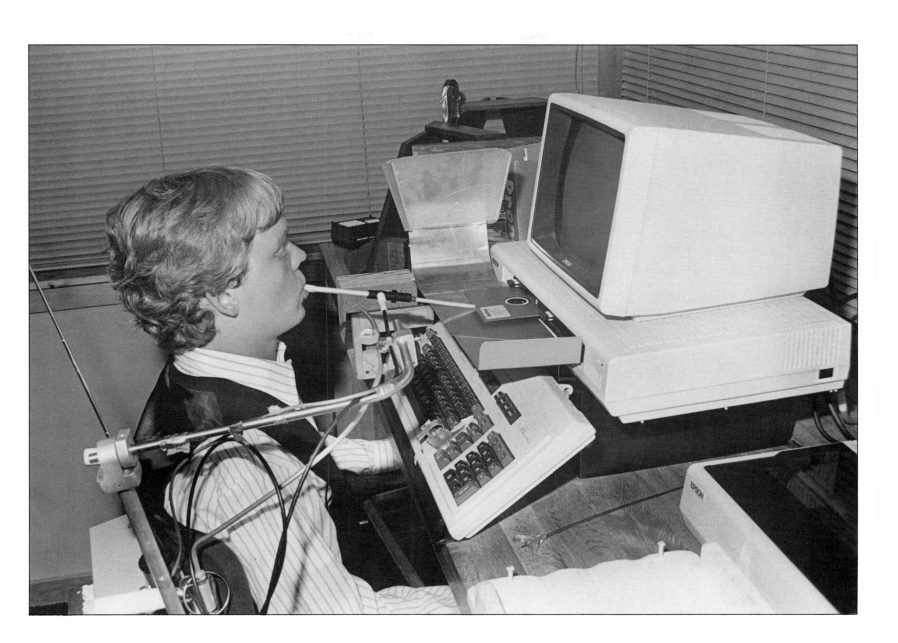

On his worktable, Greg has a stand that supports open books and magazines. One side of the stand is hinged so that it folds over and lies flat when not in use.

On top of the stand is a round magnet. Greg's magazines are fastened inside cardboard folders. At the top of each folder there is a metal

disk. On command, Willie fetches a magazine
and matches the metal disk on the folder to the
magnet on the stand. The magnet holds the
folder in place.

Next, she sets the stand in the upright
position and flips the magazine open for
Greg to read.

When Greg is thirsty he asks Willie to serve him a drink. Greg says, "Willie, door." Willie goes to the small refrigerator and opens the door. Greg aims the laser at a bottle and says, "Willie, fetch." Willie takes out the plastic juice container the light beam is hitting and carries it over to Greg's worktable. She puts the bottle into a holder anchored on the table, then unscrews the lid. Next she inserts a straw. Greg wheels himself into position in front of the straw and drinks.

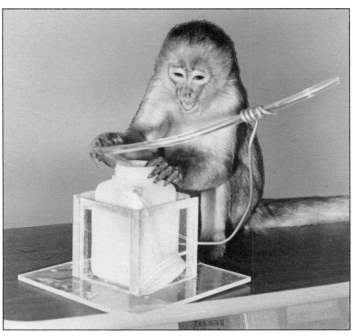
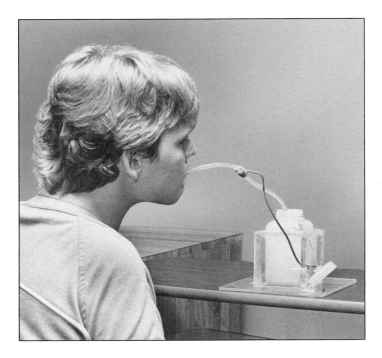

Willie also fetches sandwiches from the small refrigerator and puts them into a sandwich holder that was designed to fit on Greg's table. When the sandwich is in place, Greg can feed himself.

Occasionally Willie feeds Greg with a spoon, but usually Greg prefers human help for that. Willie sometimes tips the spoon over. And at times she forgets and feeds herself instead of Greg.

Willie has been taught to open the door of her cage, go in, and close the door behind her. If Greg wants her to go in, he says, "Willie, cage," and she obeys. When the cage door closes, it automatically locks.

At bedtime, Greg says, "Willie, cage," and she goes in. When the room is dark and she's ready to sleep, she pulls a large bath towel over herself and settles down for eight to twelve hours of rest.

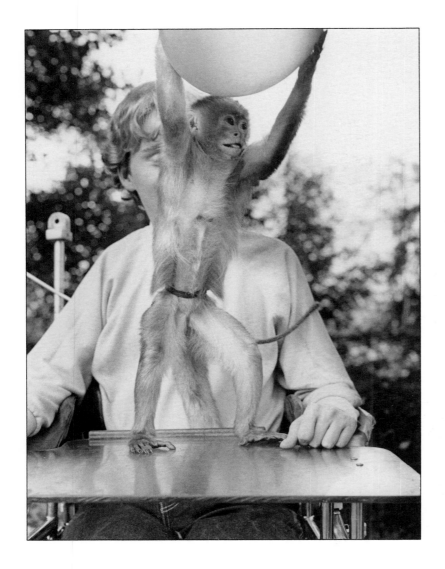 

During the day, when Greg is in his wheelchair, Willie moves about freely in the room, available to help Greg whenever he needs her. But many tasks take only a few seconds to complete, so most of Willie's time is her own.

She plays with her toys, sits on Greg's lapboard, or amuses herself with any number of activities Greg and his family have devised. Willie's favorite toys include car keys and a balloon. But she can find fun in almost anything.

A scrap of paper is to be chased around. An ice cube is interesting until it melts.

And sometimes Greg's family makes soap bubbles for Willie. She tries to catch and eat them.

There can be some unpredictable moments with a monkey living at home. Once when everyone was out of the house and the door to Willie's cage wasn't properly latched, she got out. "Willie is well fed, but she always knows where the food is," Greg says. "On that day, my brother came home and found her perched high on one of the beams in the living room. Of course he was shocked. He put Willie back in her cage and went into the kitchen. Then he was really surprised. It was a mess. The refrigerator door was open and there were smashed eggs all over the floor. All the cabinet doors were ajar and there were squashed bananas, pieces of marshmallows, and cookie crumbs on the counter. You'd better believe we always check to make sure her lock is secure when we leave the house now!"

Greg is proud of Willie and all that she can do. "She's a lot more to me than just helping hands," he says. "I spend all day, every day, in my wheelchair. One of my parents will drive me in my van to visit friends and go to ball games or movies, but a lot more of my time is spent at home than it used to be—before my accident.

"Willie gives me something to think about besides myself. When she's out of her cage, I'm always looking around to find out where she is and what she's doing."

Greg doesn't take Willie out in public. But people with quadriplegia who do take their monkeys to places like parks or shopping centers report that strangers pay greater attention to them when they are accompanied by their monkeys.

Many people have an inhibition about talking with someone in a wheelchair. They don't know quite what to say, so they don't say anything at all and ignore both the person and the chair. When a person who has quadriplegia is with a monkey, the stranger can focus attention on the monkey until he or she feels comfortable about looking at and talking directly to the person. "What is the monkey's name? What does the monkey eat? How long have you had the monkey?" These are the questions that are usually asked first. Perhaps a few more questions follow; then, before stranger and quadriplegic know it, they're having a conversation.

Greg still has the friends he had before his accident, but he's noticed that when he makes new friends, his monkey is a great help in easing the awkwardness that exists in any new friendship.

"Willie's fun to play with. She really enjoys games," says Greg. "My friends like to play catch or wrestle with her and give her treats."

There's an inseparable connection between a monkey and a person who has quadriplegia. Greg says, "If I've been out of the house, Willie is always excited and glad to see me again when I return. She looks straight at me and makes a chattering sound—a friendly greeting monkey-style. There's a real tight bond between us. From time to time, she grooms my hair—a real sign of trust and affection."

The Helping Hands organization knows how strong bonds can be. Many months after one person with quadriplegia died of a heart attack, his monkey still kissed the photograph of him that his wife kept on the bureau.

"People say to me, 'Why don't you get a robot to help you?' But did you ever see a robot that could be tender and make you laugh?" asks Greg. "Willie takes good care of me. But she's also a good friend. Life wouldn't be nearly as much fun without her."

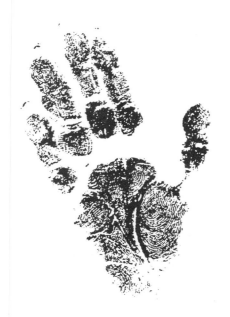

If you would like further information about the
Helping Hands program, please address your
inquiries to:

Boston University School of Medicine
HELPING HANDS
1505 Commonwealth Avenue
Boston, MA 02135

(617) 787-4419

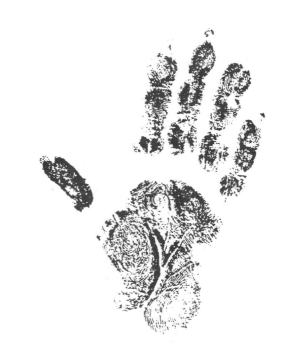